The
Magic Fish

The Fisherman and His Wife

Retold by FREYA LITTLEDALE   Pictures by ED ARNO

SCHOLASTIC BOOK SERVICES
NEW YORK · TORONTO · LONDON · AUCKLAND · SYDNEY · TOKYO

For Glenn

Text copyright © 1967 by Freya Littledale. Illustrations copyright © 1967 by Scholastic Magazines, Inc. All rights reserved. Published by Scholastic Book Services a division of Scholastic Magazines, Inc.

8th printing .... January 1972

Printed in the U.S.A.

Once upon a time there was a poor fisherman.
He lived with his wife
in an old hut by the sea.

Every day he went fishing.

One day the fisherman felt something

on the end of his line.

He pulled and he pulled.

And up came a big fish.

"Put me back in the water," said the fish.

"I am a magic fish.

I am really a prince."

"Well," said the man,
"if you are a prince,
I will put you back in the water."
And he did.

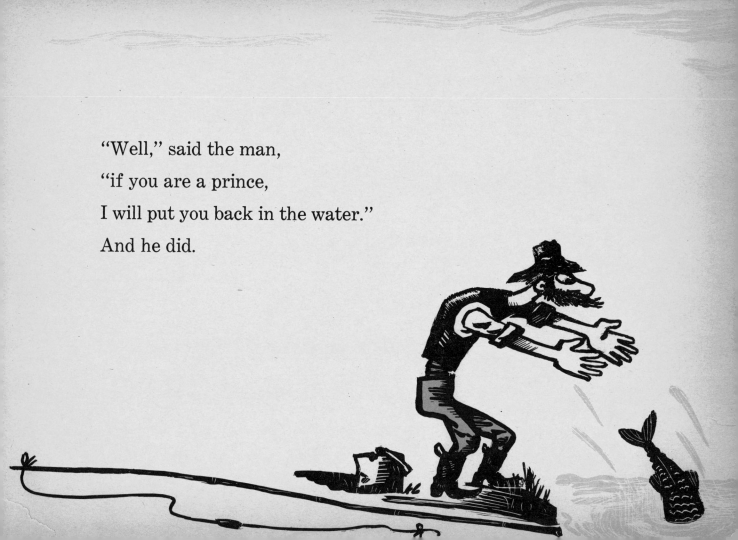

That night his wife asked him,

"Why didn't you catch any fish today?"

"I did catch a fish," said the man.

"But he was a magic fish.

He said he was really a prince.

So I let him go."

"Silly man!" said his wife.

"Why didn't you make a wish?

Go back to the fish.

Tell him I wish for a pretty house."

"Why?" asked the man.

"Never mind why," said his wife.
"Go back and tell the fish
I want a pretty house."

"I don't want to go," said the man.

"Go," said his wife.

So the fisherman went back to the sea.

The fisherman called,
"Oh, fish in the sea
Come listen to me.
My wife begs a wish
From the magic fish."

"What does she want?" asked the fish.

"She wants a pretty house," said the man.

"Go home," the fish said.

"Now your wife has a pretty house."

So the man went home.

The old hut was gone.

Now there was a pretty house.

"This is very nice," the fisherman said to his wife.

"We will be happy here."

"We shall see," said his wife.

The fisherman was happy.
His wife was happy, too.
She was happy for one week.

Then she said to the man,

"Go back to the fish.

Tell him I want more than a pretty house.

I want to live in a castle."

"Why?" asked the man.

"Never mind why," said the woman.

"Go back and tell the fish I want a castle."

"But I don't want to go," said the man.

"Go," said his wife.

So the man went back to the sea.

The man called,
"Oh, fish in the sea
Come listen to me.
My wife begs a wish
From the magic fish."

"Well," asked the fish.

"What does she want now?"

"She wants a castle," said the man.

"Go home," the fish said.
"Now your wife has a castle."

So the man went home.

The pretty house was gone.

And there was a castle.

"This is a beautiful castle," said the fisherman to his wife.

"We will be happy here."

"We shall see," said his wife.

The fisherman was happy.
And his wife was happy, too.
She was happy for two weeks.

Then she said to the fisherman,

"Go back to the fish.

Tell him I want more than the castle.

Tell him I want to be Queen of the land."

"Why?" asked the fisherman.

"Never mind why," said the woman.

"Go back to the fish and tell him

I must be Queen of the land."

"I don't want to go," said the fisherman.

"Go," said his wife.

So the man went back to the sea.

The man called,
"Oh, fish in the sea
Come listen to me.
My wife begs a wish
From the magic fish."

"Well," said the fish,
"What does she want this time?"

"She wants to be Queen of the land," said the man.

"Go home," said the fish.
"Now your wife is Queen of the land."

So the fisherman went home.

His wife was in the castle.

She was sitting on a throne made of gold.

And she wore a dress made of gold
and a crown made of gold.

"So," said the man,

"Now you are Queen of the land.

That is a fine thing to be.

At last we can be happy."

"We shall see," said his wife.

And the fisherman was happy.

His wife was happy, too.

She was happy for three weeks.

Then she said to the fisherman,
"Go back to the fish.
Tell him I want to be more
than Queen of the land.
Tell him I want to be Queen of
the sun and the moon and the stars."

"But why?" asked the fisherman.

"Never mind why," she said.
"Just go back to the fish.
Tell him I want to be Queen of
the sun and the moon and the stars."

"I don't want to go," said the man.
"The fish will be angry."

"Go," said his wife.

So the man went back to the sea.

He called,
"Oh, fish in the sea
Come listen to me.
My wife begs a wish
From the magic fish."

"What is it?" said the fish.

"She wants to be Queen of
the sun and the moon and the stars,"
said the fisherman.

"NO," said the fish.
"She wants too much.
She cannot be Queen of the sun.
She cannot be Queen of the moon and the stars.
Now she must go back to the old hut."

So the fisherman went home.

The castle was gone.

The old hut was back.

And his wife was inside.

And there they are to this very day.